Juana & Lucas

Juana
& Lucas

JUANA MEDINA

CANDLEWICK PRESS

A very big *gracias* to my editor, Mary Lee Donovan, designer
Maryellen Hanley, and editorial assistant Melanie Cordova
for their *entusiasmo* and guidance while working on this book.
I couldn't have asked for a better team.

• • •

Copyright © 2016 by Juana Medina

First paperback edition 2019

Library of Congress Catalog Card Number 2016945893
ISBN 978-0-7636-7208-9 (hardcover)
ISBN 978-1-5362-0639-5 (paperback)

19 20 21 22 23 CCP 10 9 8 7 6 5 4 3

Printed in Shenzhen, Guangdong, China

This book was typeset in Nimrod and Avenir.
The illustrations were done in ink and watercolor.

Candlewick Press
99 Dover Street
Somerville, Massachusetts 02144

visit us at www.candlewick.com

For my parents

CHAPTER 1

My name is Juana.

It's spelled

and it is pronounced

WHO-AH-NAH.

Things I like are: # Drawing.
Sometimes on paper,
sometimes on other surfaces.

Astroman.

Astroman needs no rockets to fly in space—his intergalactic suit and shiny helmet cover all of him and let him glide from galaxy to galaxy, faster than I can say Jupiter! He knows all the constellations from A to Z and can redirect a comet by simply blowing on it, as if it were a candle flame on a cupcake.

No one else can do that.

My favorite food of all foods (more than cheese and chocolate and ice cream, but not all together) is

Brussels sprouts.

In Bogotá, Brussels sprouts are called *repollitas*.

The world has many cities, but **Bogotá** is where I am. And where school is . . . and where Mami and my *abuelos* and Lucas are . . . and where I play with Eric and Daniel . . . and where I get into trouble with Juli. Bogotá, Colombia, in South America, is the city that's closest to my heart.

3

I love Bogotá.
LOVE. IT.
And here's why:

Bogotá has more NEIGHBORHOODS than I can count. There's a financial district, a flower district, galleries, houses, little coffee shops, bookstores; it just never stops. There are a lot of parks in Bogotá, too!

The *CICLOVÍA* is a never-ending route of bike lanes all across the city. I'm still learning how to ride a bike, so I haven't been able to go on every bit of bike lane across the city—it would take me ages to do it! But I like the idea of pedaling through town.

During the day, the WEATHER is mild, as if it is eternally springtime. Then the night comes, and the ground turns freezing cold, so everyone always keeps a pair of slippers by their bed.

There are many TREES, mostly old and almost as tall as buildings! In the daytime, they give shade from the incredibly strong sun. At night, when illuminated from below by the streetlights, they make shadows of all shapes and sizes.

In Bogotá, Colombia, *everyone* speaks *ESPAÑOL*! There might be a few who speak other languages, but to understand one another, we all mainly speak Spanish. Lucas doesn't speak Spanish, only because he doesn't speak at all.

At bedtime, chances are you'll find me in bed with a book . . . or *dos,* or *tres*! **Reading books** is one of my most favorite things.

Sometimes, Mami will come into my room and tell me to turn off the light ¡*ya mismo*! just when the stories I'm reading are absolutely impossible to put down.

Thank goodness my *abuelo* gave me a flashlight to use in case of an emergency. Having to turn the lights off and stop reading *inmediatamente* is definitely an emergency. I grab the flashlight, pull the covers up over my head, and go back to reading.

Even more than Astroman, even more than reading, drawing, Brussels sprouts, and Bogotá all together, I love

my furry *amigo,* Lucas.

He is the smartest and most amazing *perro* ever born. I can't think of a better friend than Lucas. He is my absolutely-no-single-doubt-about-it best *amigo.*

Some say Lucas is neurotic. I do not think so. He is actually quite calm, especially while sleeping.

I love Lucas.
LOVE. HIM.
And here's why:

Unlike others, Lucas listens to absolutely
everything I have to say, without
interrupting—even when the stories
get to be a little too long.

He jumps really high. High enough to get
cookies off the counter. Plus, he'll share
them with me!

No one is better than Lucas at
playing spies. No matter where
I hide, he always finds me.

His vision and hearing are so good that when Mami is making her way toward my room, Lucas gives me a little push with his snout, which gives me time to turn off the light. That always saves me from a talk or two about still being awake past bedtime.

Even though cleats will never fit him and gloves are pointless, he's a phenomenal goalie. He's learned from watching *fútbol* matches on TV.

He eats math homework like a pro. The harder the homework, the faster he'll eat it.

Lucas always walks me to and from the bus stop on school days, which makes the walks a lot better than what they could be.

CHAPTER 2

One day, I walk out with Lucas to wait for the school bus, and the morning is *especialmente* beautiful. The air feels clean and delicious, and smells like fresh fruit and bread, and a little bit like wet asphalt. I'm carrying my lunch box, which has a drawing of a kitty and a rabbit on it. I love it!

Often, Lucas and I have to run to the bus stop. But because today is the first day of school, we get there a little early. That means that our bus driver, Seño—who is really Señorita Cecila, but Seño is shorter—isn't mad at me and allows me to sit next to my

friend Juli.

Sitting with Juli is always good because we have *mucho* to talk about. So much that there's no time to get carsick.

Juli is a very good friend.
VERY. GOOD.

Here's what you need to know:

Juli and I have been good friends since we sat together on the school bus for the very first time—when we were five years old—and that was a very long time ago!

Sometimes all we have to do is look at each other and we'll start laughing. Sometimes we laugh until our bellies hurt. Juli has a contagious laugh.

Juli loves candy. I don't love candy as much as she does, but I do like some from time to time. Juli is such a good friend, she doesn't have trouble sharing with me.

Juli's name is Juliana, but I call her Juli because it's shorter and easier to say.

She has two brothers, one older and one younger. She's in a brother sandwich! They all live in an apartment with their parents and two dogs.

Juli is a really good swimmer. She swims better than most people I know, and I know a lot of swimmers!

This morning on the bus, Juli pulls the most fantastic pack of *delicioso* watermelon gum out of her school blazer's pocket. As soon as we figure out how to open the complicated wrappers we start chewing the neon-pink gum. The whole bus is filled with the smell of fresh sweet watermelon. It's *extraordinario*!

"Do you know how to blow bubbles out of gum?" I ask Juli.

"No. I've only seen the fifth-graders do it," she says. So we decide to try right then, and it turns out to be pretty easy! We blow bubbles as big as our *cabezas* and pop them as loud as we can. It's great fun.

Too bad Seño doesn't find this as entertaining as we do. She stops the bus and walks back to our seats. She's frowning as if a hippo just sat on her toes.

"Juana, to the back where you can sit between Santiago and Felipe," she says, pointing to two fifth-graders who are never nice to anyone. They're especially mean to kids younger than them, like me. "*Inmediatamente!*"

This day has clearly taken a turn for the worse.

Now there are rows and rows between me and Juli. In order to talk to her, I'll have to stand on my lunch box, then wave to get her attention.

But when I step up onto my lunch box, there's a loud

POP!

under my feet, and I fall right back down onto my seat. My kitty and rabbit lunch box has broken, and the yogurt inside of it has *explotado*. That's the end of my lunch and my lunch box.

The rest of the ride to school smells a little like milk and a little like strawberries, all because of my yogurt. I feel *triste*. I really liked my kitty and rabbit lunch box.

Felipe and Santiago, as mean as ever, can't stop laughing at my lunch box *tragedia*.

CHAPTER 3

I can't stop *pensando* about my crushed lunch box all morning. So when Mr. Mejía, my math teacher, says, "Juana, please come up front and solve this math equation for us," there's absolutely no chance I'll be able to figure out the answer to the *problema* scribbled on the blackboard. It's as if Mr. Mejía knew my mind was busy with other stuff.

My day is going downhill faster than an *elefante* on a skateboard, and there's still more than half a day of school left. Maybe, hopefully, things will take a sharp turn for the better. And soon!

Dance class comes right after *matemáticas* class, and it, too, is a total mess.

We're all stepping on one another's toes, the music is TOO LOUD, and we all get sweaty and red in our uncomfortable PE *uniformes*.

I may dislike the uncomfortable PE *uniforme,* but there's something a lot worse, and that is having to wear skirts and dresses. I *detesto* wearing them more than anything in the world!

Mami says, "There might be things you dislike, but at your age there's no need to detest anything." So I very strongly dislike dresses more than anything else I could possibly *detestar* in the world.

Well, almost anything. I will soon find out there are more complicated and more *frustrante* things to deal with than dresses.

I strongly dislike my uniform.
VERY. STRONGLY.
And here's why:

The blazer is heavy and hot and sometimes makes me very, very hot. Like, very-hot-celery-soup hot. It's awful.

The uniform has a tie that can make me feel like I'm choking, and that is not fun.

The skirt is itchy.

When I play on the monkey bars, I have to watch out or boys will be shouting out that my underpants are pink. I think boys should be doing better things than looking at my pink underpants.

The uniform's socks are supposed to be white, but my socks are never truly white. It's impossible to have white socks when you are a serious *fútbol* player.

Playing *fútbol* while wearing a school uniform is the worst.

It takes forever for lunchtime to come around. The cafeteria is packed, and everyone is—per usual—being scolded by Ms. Chavita.

"Children, please! Keep your hands to yourself and

stay in line!"

She has a voice that sounds like it travels from down in her high heels all the way up to her mouth. "When I was your age, everyone behaved and followed the rules!"

By the time we get our lunches, we have to gulp them down if we hope to have any time at all to play *fútbol* at recess. We run out of the cafeteria, dessert hidden in our sleeves.

I truly hope that a good game of *fútbol* at recess will help improve my day! Recess is my favorite class, and dessert is my favorite meal at school.

The *fútbol* game at recess isn't too good. Daniel isn't able to score any goals, Eric is kicked in the shin, and our one *fútbol* field is so full of people playing different games, it's hard to figure out who's playing with who.

Also, Escanilberto switches teams in the middle of the game because he thinks we're going to lose. He doesn't like losing. Once last year, he got so *furioso* about losing that he pushed David to the ground. David wound up in the infirmary with a bloody nose. Though Escanilberto is not the most fun person to be around, we need him on our side. He can kick the ball

hard enough to send it

across the field.

No one else can do that.

While nobody winds up in the infirmary with a bloody nose or bruises this time, our team loses. For once—just this once—Escanilberto was right.

CHAPTER 4

Back inside, in Mr. Tompkins's *clase,* it feels like a sauna, and after that intense *fútbol* game, this classroom is seriously stinky. Even stinkier than after dance class, and that's a lot of stinky!

We might have fallen asleep at our desks in the stuffy room if Mr. Tompkins hadn't *anunciado,*

"Ladies and gentlemen!
Are you ready for a
ton of fun?"

When a grown-up says something is going to be a ton of fun, it means there will be NO FUN AT ALL. Not even a single bit of fun. *Nada de* fun.

"My little mischiefs," he says, "today I'm going to begin teaching you something that will knock your socks off. Prepare for your lives to change . . . for the better! Today you are going to begin learning the English."

THE ENGLISH? I'm certain I don't either need or want to learn the English. I've got trouble enough already with learning math.

I feel even hotter now. And my collar itches.

Mr. Tompkins passes out books on the English. They're as big as phone books and as heavy as rocks! Inside, there are *THs* everywhere. There are also big *Ws* and long *Ls* that seem impossible to *pronunciar*.

Mr. Tompkins says, "Repeat these English words after me: 'Look. At. This. Book!'"

"Luk ad dddddizzz buuuk," I try repeating. I am good at rolling my *Rs* in Spanish—*"erre, erre, erre"*—it's easy. But I'm positively terrible at saying *thhhhh. THs* tickle my tongue.

Juli whispers, *"No entiendo nada."* I whisper back that I don't understand a thing, either. I'm glad I'm not the only one who thinks the English is *muy* hard.

Mr. Tompkins hears us. "Juana and Juliana, ¡*por favor*!" He doesn't have to finish the sentence for us to know that he wants us to stop talking and to concentrate on the English.

I wish we could all be back outside kicking the soccer ball around instead of saying words that tickle my tongue.

This day has definitely not made that turn for the better I was hoping for. Instead, it has become the worst of all first days of school possible.

When I get home from school, Mami asks about my day. I quickly tell her it was **horrible.** No, I tell her it was actually worse than horrible: my lunch box broke, my yogurt exploded, we lost our *fútbol* game, it was hot, everyone was stinky, my collar itched, and, worst of all, Mr. Tompkins said we have to learn the English. Truly, a day doesn't get worse than that.

Mami is the most important person in my life.
MOST. IMPORTANT.
And here's why:

Mami is very brave and strong. When I was a tiny baby, my father died in a fire. It was an awful accident. This made Mami very sad, but she always shows me how important it is to find happiness, no matter what, even in the littlest things.

Besides being the best of moms, Mami is really good at taking care of plants. She loves all plants, even the ones with complicated names I can't pronounce.

If there could be a champion of paper-airplane making, it would be Mami.

There's no better cook or baker in the world than Mami.

No one smells as good as Mami. She always smells fresh as mint, warm as cinnamon, and just like the soft jasmine flowers that bloom late at night.

Mami says, "Juana, I know it's hard to believe, but learning English *can* change your life . . . in a good way." Mami agrees with Mr. Tompkins? How could this possibly be? I quickly point out how, despite today being the worst day of all worst days, my life is pretty fantastic and that the English will do nothing but ruin it.

"Well, Juana, if you don't believe me, maybe you should ask a few other people why you should learn English."

Should. Should. Should.

Should is the least fun word in the dictionary.

If there's anyone who knows how to turn my life around for the better, it's Lucas. "Don't you think life is already wonderful without my needing to learn the English?" I ask him. Lucas yelps and licks my face. Good *respuesta*!

Lucas is the only cure for a HORRIBLE day.

CHAPTER 5

Days and days of English lessons have not made it any easier to speak it. My tongue still tickles with all the *TH*s . . .

in THumb, THimble, THick,

THorn, and THird.

And it is increasingly hard to remember all the words I should know by now.

Left,   right,

UP,

DOWN,

above,

below,

behind . . .

All the words are as hard as it gets. Why not just speak in Spanish? It is SO much easier!

Our neighbors from across the hall, Mr. Sheldon and Mrs. Sheldon, are very, very old. Maybe one hundred and forty-five years old. They grew up in a faraway country across the gigantic *Océano* Atlantic. But they've been living in Colombia for the longest time. Maybe the Sheldons will know of at least one good reason for me to learn the English.

Mrs. Sheldon, as always, asks me to take my shoes off on entering their *apartamento*. (Which is too bad, because I think stepping on the thick white carpets with my *fútbol* shoes would feel so comfortable!)

Mr. Sheldon knows a lot about everything. Not a little about all, but a lot about everything! So I think it's a good idea to ask him about the English. "Mr. Sheldon, is there a single good reason for me to be tortured to learn the English?"

"*Well, of course!* Learning English is imperative in helping our nation develop in a global economy," he says.

I don't understand a single bit of what that means. It sounds almost as complicated as the English.

There's no way the English will change my life for the better, no matter what Mr. Tompkins or Mami or Mr. Sheldon says.

On Friday after school I decide to take Lucas out for a walk to visit the Herrera brothers and ask about this English situation.

Mami says the Herrera brothers bicker like an old married couple, but I really like them. They always let Lucas into their shop, and their shop smells of oranges and cloves. The Herrera brothers' shop is also small, almost too small for both very big brothers to fit inside at the same time!

While eating a fresh and crunchy *empanada,* I ask them what they think about me having to learn the English.

"We think it's *fantástico*!"

"You could help us translate all our store signs into English so tourists can understand what we're selling!" adds Fernando.

"That is the best idea I've heard from my brother in thirty years!" says Hernando.

Thirty years is a *loooong* time to have only one good idea, and quite frankly, I don't even think it's that good. *Primero,* I have never in my entire long life seen a tourist walk into the Herrera brothers' shop. *Segundo,* the brothers' shop is puny. If all the signs were written in

español <u>and</u> English

there'd be no space left for anyone to go inside.

After all the asking, I still have not heard one single convincing reason for me to learn the English.

CHAPTER **6**

There are days when the English is not my only trouble. On Monday, I forget to bring in my math homework, so Mr. Mejía asks me to go up to the blackboard to solve the *problemas* he had assigned in front of the whole class.

By the time I get to Mr. Tompkins's class, my brain cannot hold another thought—not even one in Spanish.

In the scorching-hot classroom, Mr. Tompkins explains things about the English that make very little sense to me. Why are *read* and *read* written the same way but sound different? How can I know when people are talking about *eyes* or *ice* when they sound about the same? And what about *left* hand and *left* the room? So many words, so little sense.

While everyone is sitting in *silencio* and paying close attention to what Mr. Tompkins is reading, I try to peek at the next page to see how much reading is left. I try doing it fast and quietly, but what happens fast and not very quietly is that I get the most painful paper cut a page of an English book could have ever caused. I let go of an

"*¡Ayayay!*"

Mr. Tompkins shoots me a look and says, "Juana, in English it's *Ouch*, not *¡Ayayay!*"

After school, Mami comes to pick me up so we can visit
Tía Cristina. Which is great news, because I'm sure Tía
Cris will tell Mami that it's not necessary for me to learn
the English, and we'll move on to more pleasant things.

There's absolutely no chance Tía Cris will think I need
to learn more of the English. Especially after it has hurt
me deeply and even required a Band-Aid!

Tía Cris is my favorite aunt.
OF. ALL. AUNTS.
And here's why:

Tía Cris has the most *fantástica* music collection I've ever seen . . . or heard! In her collection, there are songs about blue *unicornios* and fishermen stealing stars, and even some tunes about houses built on clouds.

She's a potter, and in her house, there are not only beautiful ceramic pots she's made, which hold flowers and paintbrushes and fruit, but portraits and books and posters from all over the world.

No matter how sad one might be, Tía Cris can make the saddest of all days a happy one.

It turns out that Tía Cris knows A LOT of the English. She also tells me, "The best reason to learn English is to be able to sing a lot of great songs." I already know plenty of songs to *cantar* in Spanish.

The day becomes dark and gloomy then, and it starts pouring, as if the sky has suddenly become the sea and it's falling over Bogotá, all at once.

CHAPTER 7

Tonight, right when I'm about to turn the page to learn what will happen to the hero of my book, Mami comes in, takes away my flashlight, and gives me a kiss. "Close your eyes and go to sleep. It's late," she says, tucking me in.

Now my room is really dark, but through the *ventana,* I can see the Andes Mountains surrounding the city, giving Bogotá a giant hug.

I can also see the stars above and the stars below. Mami says the stars are only above, and that what I see below are simply city lights. The lights go on so far into the distance, it looks as if the city is wrapped

Mami has a smile as bright as the stars above and below Bogotá, but when she's mad, her eyes turn greener than all of the Andes put together. Fortunately, she doesn't get mad very often, but parent-teacher conferences are tomorrow. To be quite honest, things are not looking good. At. All. I'm afraid Mami won't be too happy by the end of the day tomorrow.

Even though Lucas is sleeping, he is moving his legs *muy* fast. He is also snoring like a jet plane. No friend, no matter how good they are, should snore this loud so close to your ears. You would think Lucas's sleepiness would help me to fall asleep, but all I can seem to do is yawn.

And all this yawning is certainly making me thirsty.
Falling asleep at night can be hard sometimes. I wonder if
I should get up to ask Mami for a glass of *agua*.

CHAPTER **8**

I knew this day would come, and I knew
it wouldn't be pretty.

It's parent-teacher conference day, and my grades will
most definitely not be the best. It's just so hard to remember all the English I'm supposed to know when there's
fútbol to play and fun to be had.

After school is over, my *abuelos* will pick me up so Mami can talk to Mr. Tompkins. After seeing my grades, Mami will most definitely not be happy. Thank goodness I will be with Abue and Abuelita at their house all afternoon. That will delay a little bit the very serious *conversación* I'll be having about my report card with Mami. As if they knew I'd be needing him, my *abuelos* picked up Lucas from home and brought him along, too.

They live in a house that is *perfecta.* It has all the space they need but not more, so you always feel welcome, but you never feel lost. Inside the *casa,* they have space for Abuelita's carpentry projects and space for Abuelito's books. They have a beautiful garden with roses and a big magnolia tree. They have bird feeders and some carved rocks where there's always fresh water for birds to take baths in.

My *abuelos'* casa is *perfecta* because it has everything we need to be happy. There are always things to do, like draw maps or read about the Etruscans or trace designs on wood for Abuelita to cut out perfectly.

They also have a yellow mug for me when I come over. They serve me really cold water to cool off, especially when I come in red as a *manzana* from playing *fútbol* outside.

Out of my absolute favorite people in all the world, my *abuelos* are two of my very top *favoritos*.

I call my *abuelo* Abue because it's shorter and faster to say. Almost everyone else calls him Dr. Rosas.

Abue is the greatest!
THE. GREATEST.
And here's why:

No one in the whole wide world loves chocolate as much as Abue does. He has a secret drawer packed with chocolate in his library. I'm the only one who knows which the secret drawer is.

Abue also loves dogs. There are always dog treats in his pockets!

Abue is a neurosurgeon. That's a very complicated word that means he is a doctor who does brain surgery.

When someone asks him what he does for a living, he says he is a student. Which is true! He sits with his books and we do homework together for hours.

Abue has a *maletín* in which he carries amazing pens, plenty of books, and papers full of squiggly lines that make no sense to me.

In Abue's library, I sit on his lap. While we eat choco-
lates, I tell him my problems, which, like chocolate, seem
to melt a w a y .

But then I tell him about the English. At first he just
listens and listens to all I say. "No matter how hard I try,"
I tell him, "there's always more and more to learn and
to practice. It all seems so pointless. When it comes to the
English, it never seems to get any easier."

Finally, he smiles and says, "Juani"—Abue and Abuelita call me Juani; I like that—"when I was in medical school in Chicago, everyone only spoke English to me. The same thing happened to me in New Orleans. And guess what? It was the same in Boston, too!"

There's an old globe in Abue's library. On it, he shows me where Bogotá is. He also points out Chicago and New Orleans and Boston—all faraway places where he studied and all places where they speak English. Turns out, Abue doesn't just know how to speak English, he LOVES it. He loves Spanish, too, but tells me that English has been an important tool to him for a very long time. That's the language he used in all those cities to learn more about the brain, to make great friends, and to read almost all the books in his massive library.

This makes my head spin more than the old globe.

"But do you want to know the best reason to learn English?" he asks. He takes out a calendar. He flips some pages and then points to some dates. "On these days," he says, "I'm taking you to Spaceland. At Spaceland they only speak English. No one speaks Spanish. Not even Astroman."

My goodness. Abue is taking Mami and Abuelita and me to *Spaceland!*

The real Spaceland! The one in Orlando, Florida, U.S. of A. Where the one and only Astroman lives! It will take one long flight on a very big plane for us to get there, and it will mean Lucas staying over with the Sheldons, but the Sheldons are nice so it's okay.

Now I must learn all the English I can so I can *hablar* with Astroman in *Spaceland.*

Spaceland is like a universe but in a single little town. It has buildings that look like planets, and you're transported in shooting stars that are really just little cars that look like shooting stars, and there's a 3-D planetarium and spinning asteroid bumper cars. . . . I've never been there, but I've read all about it.

This day is now the worst AND the greatest of all days.

CHAPTER 9

Just as I feared, Mami and I have a very serious talk about my grades. She says it's absolutely *necesario* for me to improve my grades or there will be

NO visit to Spaceland.

From then on, I eat the English, drink the English, even gargle the English. Who thinks of naming *leche* "milk"? It's so hard to say! And what about "shoelace"? It's much easier to say *cordón*! "Flapjack" is a seriously odd word, and let's not even talk about "silverware" or "horseplay." I can't even start to spell "wristwatch," though I want one very badly for my birthday.

I work *muy, muy* hard to learn *todo* the English that I can possibly fit into the

space between my pigtails.

Before Mr. Tompkins, Mami, the Sheldons, the Herrera brothers, Tía Cris, and my *abuelos* can believe it, I am a big and loud fountain of English. Even Lucas is surprised at how quickly I have learned to speak this new language.

I read English books aloud with Mr. Sheldon. We read about Ramona and little bits of Harriet. We try at times to read Shakespeare, but I can barely even pronounce his name! And we read some Jules Verne stories, even though he wrote them in French and someone decided to make their life miserable and translate them ALL into English.

It was dark, and very hard to see past their

It was a quiet evening on a pleasant summer night. . . .

The tide was high, making their ship appear to be a small speck. . . .

She knew this would work as expected, what she didn't know . . .

noses. . . . .

Now I have English in my *cabeza,* as if it were an open toolbox—not too heavy and always at hand.

I help the Herrera brothers translate signs. At the _{teeny-tiny} *mercado,* everything now has a label in two languages: Spanish and English.

Tía Cris and I sing songs about yellow submarines, and we sing a sad song about a whale and a bird, and a song about dancing with ourselves, oh, oh . . . and we sing them all loud! Louder than her power

ful stereo system.

When Escanilberto pulls my hair, I tell him exactly what I think *in English*. I tell him that there's absolutely no reason whatsoever for him to even come *close* to my hair. And if he does, with the **strength of Thor** **and** **the speed of ninjas,** I will

send him directly to the moon!

Or at least to Principal Mrs. Leon's office.

He cannot stand not knowing what I am saying! But he knows it's better for him not to bother me or he'll be in trouble.

I can see the days Abue circled on the *calendario* getting closer and closer.

It's almost time for our trip to Spaceland!

12

19

24

26

21

1

7

8

CHAPTER 10

I help Mami prepare for our trip. *Especialmente*
by carefully choosing the books I'll take with me and by
making sure that my sneakers are comfortable enough for
a lot of walking. The best way to do this is to wear my
sneakers all the time around the *apartamento*.

It is a true shame Lucas can't go with us. It's not easy
to leave my best friend behind.

I'd like for him to go with me and experience Spaceland firsthand, especially meeting Astroman! We could ride the bumper cars together, and fly in the zero-gravity chamber, and bounce around wearing lunar shoes, and *comer* Astro ice cream. . . .

But he'll be fine with the Sheldons while I do all those things with my *abuelos* and Mami.

Off we go to SPACELAND, finalmente!

From our plane up in the sky, we can see the big Andes Mountains, some *volcanes,* and silvery lakes. The majestic Magdalena River extends forever. It looks like a giant arm reaching out with the tips of its fingers to touch the warm *océano.*

The tops of the Sierra Nevada, peeking through the heavy clouds, wave good-bye to us as we keep on traveling north over the bluest waters one can see from the sky. Abuelita tells me the name of everything below, while Abue takes a nap that lasts as long as it takes for us to

fly over

the ocean.

It is a long *viaje,* but that's okay, because Mami gives me apple-flavored gum and I get to read my book about adventurers traveling to the center of the earth, which makes our trip seem a lot shorter.

After I've drawn, colored, watched a little bit of a movie, taken a short nap, and eaten a few snacks, we finally get to the U.S. of A. That stands for United States of America. I like that name—everyone seems united in one **BIG** America.

CHAPTER 11

Spaceland is beautiful! It's as big as a city.

It has *parques* and gardens, waterfalls, big bright buildings shaped like *planetas,* and a big and shiny one shaped like a rocket.

I can't wait to meet

There are things to do all day and all night at Spaceland. I haven't seen Astroman yet, but I've been very busy, using all my English by making conversation with the hotel manager, with people dressed up as extraterrestrials, with people waiting in line to get on the meteor rides, and with Mr. B. the waiter, who brings me a huge Astro ice cream with one Saturn cherry on top.

After walking and walking and *caminando* some more,
I suddenly see Astroman. He's really tall!

I run to him

as *rápido*

as I can.

I give him a big *abrazo,* and despite his big and techie intergalactic suit and his gigantic space helmet, he hugs me right back.

"Astroman! Guess what? I learned English so that I can talk to you!" And then I show him. I use the *THs* that tickle my tongue, I use the *Ls* that are long and hard to say. I tell Astroman about Lucas, and about my *abuelos,* and about Eric and Daniel and Juli, and I even tell him about Mr. Tompkins and Escanilberto!

. . . and then I went to visit
Mr. and Mrs. Sheldon . . .

. . . but before I could kick the ball,
Escanilberto jumped and . . .

Mr. Tompkins also told us about . . .

My mom bought me these socks that . . .

Lucas is tall but not so tall and he is
really the best companion ever.
Do you have a dog, Astroman?

Abue and Abuelita helped me look
for you all over Spaceland, until . . .

I should tell you more about Bogotá
and maybe you could visit on your . . .

The Herrera brothers got little signs that could fit
in their tiny store. Maybe you can buy
your vegetables in their store when
you visit Colombia. . . .

I wonder if you could get to Mars
with your special suit. . . .

Does your mom make you do your homework
before coming to Spaceland to play?

I talk to Astroman in English until I run out of breath. Finally, I stop *hablando* and wait for Astroman to say something back to me.

Instead, he gives me another big *abrazo* and then
turns to hug someone else.

Abue was right. Astroman doesn't *habla* Spanish. But he doesn't speak English, either. It turns out, Astroman doesn't speak at all!

For a couple of *minutos* I feel like I've learned English for absolutely *nada*. After I worked so hard to tell Astroman about my fantastic life, he didn't even say "Peep" back to me.

Still, maybe it wasn't such a bad idea to learn all this English. After all, it brought me here to Spaceland with Abue and Mami and Abuelita to eat a lot of ice cream and to go on all the fun rides.

And the number-one thing I've learned from coming here to Spaceland in Florida in the U.S. of A. is that I'd love to keep on traveling! Even if Astroman didn't seem to care much about my stories, other people did. Because I can speak English so well, I've been able to have fun with a lot of new people and make a lot of new friends. And who wouldn't like for that to happen

all around the world?

The number-two thing I've learned is that if I want to travel and make new friends, I will need to learn a gazillion more languages besides English and *español*! That's what Abue says.

I don't know if there will be enough *espacio* between my pigtails for French and Chinese and Italian and Farsi and Portuguese and all the other languages. Maybe it's time to go back to Colombia and ask Lucas what he thinks about that.

Juana's life is just about perfect.
Lately, though,
things have become a little less perfect.

Mami has been doing her hair differently, wearing more perfume, and singing *canciones*. Mami also has a new friend named Luis. Lately, Mami has been spending a lot of time with Luis. A LOT.

Juana should have known the moment she saw Mami's new hairdo that they were in for big *problemas*. BIG.

Available in hardcover and audio

www.candlewick.com